## The Beekman

Imitating the movie, Kate pointed a finger in Patti's direction. "Goodwoman Jenkins," she said in a screechy voice, "I curse you, and your sons, and your sons' sons, to an eternity of ill luck." Then she broke into giggles. "I mean, who could take that seriously?"

After everything that went on at the sleepover, I couldn't help thinking of . . . the *Beekman curse.* What if Kate's words were right, and the time was right, and the moon and stars were in the right places? Anything is possible.

Especially after what happened on Monday.

**Look for these and other books
in the Sleepover Friends Series:**

#1  *Patti's Luck*

#2  *Starring Stephanie*

# Patti's Luck

## Susan Saunders

AN
**APPLE**
PAPERBACK

SCHOLASTIC INC.
New York Toronto London Auckland Sydney

ISBN 0-590-40641-8

12 11 10 9 8 7 6                                              9/8 0 1 2/9

Printed in the U.S.A.                                              11

First Scholastic printing, August 1987

*For Heidi and Jenny*

# Patti's Luck

# Chapter 1

"So — what did you think of her?" Stephanie Green asked, between bites of an eggroll.

"Think of whom?" Kate Beekman said. She was digging around with two chopsticks in a big Chinese takeout carton of fried rice. She pulled out a piece of pork and popped it in her mouth.

"Patti Jenkins, of course!" Stephanie said. "Did you like her?"

"It's kind of hard to decide if you like somebody based on twenty minutes in the school cafeteria," Kate answered. "The boys were making so much noise, I could barely hear her."

"What did you think of her, Lauren?"

That's me — Lauren Hunter. I stopped gnawing

on a barbecued sparerib long enough to say, "She seemed really shy."

"She'll get over that. You're both going to like her a lot," Stephanie said firmly. "I still can't believe it. Somebody I used to know back in the city actually turning up in Mrs. Mead's class at Riverhurst Elementary, of all places!"

"Of all places!" Kate echoed, raising an eyebrow at me.

"Oh, not that there's anything wrong with Riverhurst Elementary," Stephanie said breezily. "It's just that — "

"It's just incredible that anyone from the city could even find Riverhurst, it's so far out in the sticks," Kate drawled. "Much less be living here and going to school at Riverhurst Elementary."

Stephanie lived in the city until the summer before fourth grade. Kate says Stephanie's always trying to prove she's light-years ahead of the country clods — meaning Kate and me. But I think it's just that Stephanie already had her own way of doing things before she moved here, and it's taking Kate a while to get used to it.

"Come on, you guys — cut it out," I said almost automatically.

According to my older brother, Roger, Kate and Stephanie argue because they're both bossy, and each of them believes she knows best.

"You know what's incredible?" I added. "That we're *fifth*-graders!"

It was Friday night. We'd just finished our first week of fifth grade. (Friday had been Patti Jenkins's first day, because she'd had some sort of trouble registering.) Stephanie and I were at Kate's house for one of our regular Friday-night sleepovers.

"Fifth-graders," Kate said slowly, rolling the words around on her tongue. "Doesn't that sound a lot more mature than *fourth*-graders?"

"Kate!" Melissa, Kate's little sister, shrieked through the closed door to Kate's bedroom. "Can I come in?"

Mrs. Beekman had let us bring our Chinese food upstairs so we could talk in peace, without interruptions from nosy Melissa. But Melissa never gives up.

"No — go away!" Kate ordered.

"You'd better not get any Moo-shu sauce on the floor," Melissa warned. "Mom just had it polished."

Talk about bossy!

"Please get out of here!" Kate yelled.

3

Melissa made a rude noise and stamped down the hall.

"You don't know how lucky you are to be an only child," Kate said grimly to Stephanie.

"Are there any dumplings left?" I asked.

"More dumplings?" Stephanie exclaimed. "You eat like a horse, Lauren — why don't you gain weight? It isn't fair," she added, sucking in her cheeks to make hollows.

Stephanie worries that her face is too round.

"I jog with Roger four times a week," I said, spearing the last dumpling with my chopsticks. "It's great — you ought to try it."

"It's great for jocks. I tried jogging once," Kate told Stephanie. "It nearly killed me! I was crippled for days."

I guess Kate and I are best friends because we've agreed to disagree. For instance, I like sports, and Kate really doesn't.

"Jogging makes me sweat," Stephanie said. "And sweating makes my hair frizz."

Stephanie has dark curly hair that she's let grow since first grade.

"I wish I had that problem for a change," I said, looking at a piece of my own straggly brown hair.

"You want curls?" Stephanie said. "Get your hair wet under the faucet. Kate, could I have a comb and some rubber bands, please."

"What are you going to do with rubber bands?" Kate asked, opening her desk and taking out a box.

"Braid Lauren's hair," Stephanie answered as I raced into the bathroom.

Kate's blonde hair is short, and she wears it brushed back from her face. It always looks neat. Her room is impossibly neat, too. She pulls open a drawer, and bingo — she finds rubber bands, right where they're supposed to be. Some days my room is so messy that I'm lucky if I can find my *desk*.

I sat on the floor of Kate's bedroom with a towel around my shoulders, and Stephanie started making tiny braids all over my head. She fastened each one with a rubber band. "When your hair is dry, we'll comb it out and you'll have thousands of little waves."

"Where'd you learn this?" I asked her.

"In the city, from my friend Tiffany's older sister. She's a model," Stephanie answered as she braided. "She always braids her hair the night before a shoot."

Kate poked me with her toe and rolled her eyes: Not the city again, I could practically hear her thinking.

But I like hearing about the people Stephanie knew there, and the plays she's seen, and the party she went to at a roller disco, and the time she bumped right into Chris Evert Lloyd, the tennis star, on the street in front of her apartment. I certainly never bumped into anyone famous on my street in Riverhurst.

"Does Patti Jenkins know Tiffany?" I asked.

Stephanie shook her head. "No, Patti stopped going to my school after first grade, when her family moved across town. That's why I didn't recognize her at first. I hadn't seen her in three and a half years."

It wasn't until our teacher, Mrs. Mead, introduced Patti to the class that Stephanie realized who Patti was — and the other way around.

"I'm Patti Jenkins," the new girl had said softly, looking nervous and uncomfortable. She was tall and thin, with brownish hair pulled straight back in a clip.

"Patti Jenkins?" Stephanie had blurted. "From the Lucretia Mott School in the city?"

"Uh, yes," the girl answered, sounding startled. "I went to Lucretia Mott."

"Stephanie Green — remember me?"

The girl stared at Stephanie with a puzzled expression.

"Mrs. Vella's room," Stephanie prompted. "We sat next to the aquarium?"

At last the girl's face broke into a shy smile. "Stephanie Green," she said, finally recognizing her.

"There, Patti," Mrs. Mead nodded approvingly. "You've found an old friend, and you'll soon make many new ones."

Stephanie wanted Patti to become part of our group right away. But Kate doesn't like to rush into things.

For years it was just Kate and me. We've been best friends since kindergarten. In those days, sleepovers meant Kool Pops, dressing up in our moms' clothes, and playing school. Kate's dad named us the Sleepover Twins.

As we got older, we moved up to eating an onion-soup-olives-bacon-bits-and-sour-cream dip I invented, along with crates of barbecue potato chips, drinking Dr. Peppers, writing Mad Libs, spying on my brother and his friends at my house, and avoiding Melissa at Kate's. But it was still just the two of us: Kate and me.

Then Stephanie and I got to be friends in Room 4A, Mr. Civello's fourth-grade class. We visited back and forth on Pine Street, which is where Kate, Stephanie, and I all live. But it wasn't until I'd known Stephanie for a few months that I asked her to one of our sleepovers. Then she invited Kate and me to her house — her mother makes great peanut-butter chocolate-chip cookies — and the three of us started hanging around together on weekends. We went to movies, shopped at the mall, and practiced dancing to MTV — Stephanie's a great dancer. Little by little, the Sleepover Twins became a threesome.

But *four* of us? It was really too soon to even think about it.

"I wouldn't have expected her to be so tall," Stephanie was saying. "Patti was the shortest girl in first grade. Now she's the tallest girl in fifth grade."

As far as I was concerned, that was definitely a point in Patti's favor. I've gotten pretty tall myself in the past year, and I thought it might be nice not to feel like the giant of the group.

There was a knock on the door, and Kate's mom stuck her head into the room. "Girls, please try to keep it down tonight — Dr. Beekman had a rough day at the hospital, and he's exhausted. Okay?"

"Sure, Mom," Kate said.

"We will, Mrs. Beekman," Stephanie and I chimed in.

"Good night," said Mrs. Beekman. "Interesting hairdo, Lauren," she added with a doubtful glance at my head.

"Finished!" said Stephanie, wrapping a rubber band around the bottom of the last braid.

Kate giggled. "If there were olives on the ends of those, you'd look sort of like a cheese ball stuck with toothpicks."

The words "cheese ball" made me hungry again. "Any snacks downstairs?"

"I made fudge after school," Kate said. "It's in the refrigerator — come on." Kate's fudge is half chocolate and half marshmallow fluff — it's terrific.

Before she opened her bedroom door, she added, "Whatever you do, don't wake up Melissa, or we'll never hear the end of it."

We tiptoed down the dark stairs to the kitchen for the fudge. Kate carried the pan into the living room and turned the TV on low. A bunch of people were standing around in sandals and togas.

"All right! 'Film Classics'!" Kate said.

Kate is a real movie freak: comedies, science

fiction, silents, foreign movies — you name it, she'll watch it. She'd like to be a movie director some day.

Stephanie loves movies, too, but it's the acting that interests her. "The girl in the blue robe sounds just like Jenny Carlin," Stephanie said.

"Can you believe the way Jenny practically drools all over Pete Stone?" said Kate. "It's embarrassing."

Jenny and Pete are in Mrs. Mead's class, too.

"Ooooh, Pete — you're so funnnny!" Stephanie said, her teeth clenched together, mimicking Jenny perfectly. "Who does Pete like?" she asked in her own voice.

"Last year he liked Tracy Osner," I answered. "But now Tracy likes Alan Reese."

"Pete's kind of cute. And he's tall, Lauren," Stephanie pointed out.

I shrugged. "Pete Stone doesn't do anything for me."

"He's even tall enough for Patti," Stephanie said thoughtfully.

"This movie is dubbed!" Kate muttered. "Their voices are saying one thing, and their lips are saying something else — that drives me crazy!"

"Why don't you turn it off? We can always play Truth or Dare," Stephanie suggested.

"Let's!" I agreed.

Kate switched off the television.

"I'll start," Stephanie said. "Kate — truth or dare?"

The last time Kate said "dare" to Stephanie, she ended up having to call the nerdiest boy in Riverhurst — Robert Ellwanger — and ask him over. Thank goodness he said no.

I wasn't surprised when Kate replied, "Truth."

"Oka-a-ay," said Stephanie. "Which boy in our class do you like best?"

"In Mrs. Mead's room?" Kate said cagily, trying to throw Stephanie off the track — Kate doesn't especially like anybody in Mrs. Mead's room. "Oh, probably . . ."

"No, no — in the *whole* fifth grade," Stephanie interrupted.

"Well . . . uh . . ." Kate blushed. "I guess . . . Bobby Krieger."

"Bobby Krieger?" Stephanie squealed.

"Sssh!" Kate warned.

"You're kidding!" Stephanie whispered.

"No, I'm not kidding," Kate replied testily.

"Bobby Krieger has red hair," Stephanie said.

"So what?" Kate growled.

"Don't you think red hair on boys is kind of . . . icky?" said Stephanie.

"Not as icky as big — "

"I think Bobby is really cute," I blurted out, before Kate could say "ears." Larry Jackson, one of the boys Stephanie likes, has ears that stick way out, but she doesn't seem to notice them. "It's your turn, Kate."

"Lauren, truth or dare?" Kate said, still frowning at Stephanie.

"Dare," I answered. Dares are scarier, but more fun.

"Hmmm." Kate was thinking. "I dare you to . . . knock on Donald's window!"

"Donald Foster?" I squeaked.

I live two houses down from Kate, and Donald Foster lives in the house between us. He's in the seventh grade, he's really good-looking, and he thinks he's the most wonderful thing that ever happened to girls.

"You chose dare," Kate said sweetly.

She and Stephanie grinned at me.

"I can't go outside like this!" I said, tugging at two rubber bands.

"Don't pull those out!" Stephanie said. "Your

hair is still wet. You want all my work to go down the tubes?"

"Stop stalling, Lauren," said Kate.

She led Stephanie and me into the kitchen again, and opened the back door as quietly as she could.

I groaned. "Some of the lights are still on at the Fosters!"

"Donald's room is dark," Kate said.

"It's not!" I told her. "His room is the third window from the end."

A dim light glowed through the curtains behind the third window.

"Maybe he sleeps with a night-light on," Stephanie snickered.

"Go ahead," Kate said to me.

At least I had one thing to be grateful for — I hadn't changed into my nightshirt yet. I took a deep breath . . . then I walked slowly down the back steps and crept across the Beekmans' lawn, my eyes fixed on Donald Foster's lighted window.

There's a hedge between the Beekmans and the Fosters. I squeezed through it, my heart practically stopping as the twigs rustled and snapped. I slipped up to the third window, I reached out . . . I knocked on it!

Okay — I didn't exactly *knock* on it. But I did tap it — once — lightly. Then I crashed through the hedge into the Beekmans' backyard. It was right about then that somebody shrieked!

I was afraid to look behind me. "Was that Donald Foster?" I gasped as I leaped up the back steps.

Kate pulled me inside. "No. It's Melissa!" she hissed. "Quick — into the living room and turn on the TV."

Melissa was making all kinds of noise upstairs. "I saw it, Mommy — I saw a space creature!"

A space creature?

Stephanie and Kate peered at me in the flickering light from the television set.

"It had this huge head, with antennas — and it was right outside!" Melissa was insisting.

"Your hair!" Kate muttered.

She and Stephanie worked fast. By the time Mrs. Beekman got downstairs, they'd pulled out all the rubber bands. My head was looking more or less earthlike. And it was absolutely covered with wild, kinky curls!

"Hi, Mom," Kate said innocently. "What's Melissa yelling about?"

"She says she saw a space creature in the backyard." Mrs. Beekman sighed. "You girls wouldn't know anything about that, would you?"

"Probably a nightmare," Kate replied. "We've just been sitting here watching TV." With a straight face, she added, "We didn't hear any flying saucers landing."

Mrs. Beekman gazed at us sleepily. "I guess you're right — Melissa was having a nightmare," she said finally. "Your hair looks lovely, Lauren — good night, all."

When she was safely upstairs, we cracked up.

"Lauren — a space creature!" Kate giggled.

"It's definitely an improvement over a cheese ball, thanks very much." I made a face at her.

We decided to postpone Truth or Dare until next time, since Melissa was probably going to be on the lookout for more space creatures.

Before we fell asleep, Stephanie murmured, "I think Patti would have had a great time tonight."

# Chapter
## 2

My hair looked terrific Saturday and Sunday, but by Monday morning after I washed it, it was back to its usual limp self. We learned a little more about Patti that day — mostly from Stephanie, since Patti wasn't much of a talker.

Both of Patti's parents are history professors, and they are teaching at the university here. She has a little brother named Horace. She's smart — she learned to read when she was three.

"When did you move to Riverhurst?" I asked her over a lunch of mystery meat in the school cafeteria.

"A month ago," Patti answered in her soft voice.

"Her house is on Mill Road," Stephanie added.

"That's only about four blocks from where we live," Kate told Patti.

"You can ride to school with us," I said. "Do you have a bike?"

Patti nodded. "But I haven't ridden it much, since I don't really know my way around yet."

"Hey!" said Stephanie. "The Pine Streeters — Lauren, Kate, and I — can show you around Riverhurst this Friday . . . then the four of us can sleep over at my house."

You have to hand it to Stephanie — she worked the sleepover in pretty neatly.

"I'd like that," said Patti shyly.

But we'd already planned to spend Friday night at my house. Kate wanted to watch two old sci-fi movies on Channel 24. We were going to make butterscotch popcorn. Kate was bringing a plate of her special fudge. Stephanie knew all that, of course — she was coming, too.

"Uh, what about the sci-fi double feature we were planning to watch at my house?" I asked, glancing nervously at Kate.

"We can do it at my house," Stephanie urged.

Patti looked crushed when it seemed as though things might not work out.

"Okay." Kate gave in, shrugging a shoulder.

"Fine with me," I said.

"Then it's settled!" said Stephanie.

Patti smiled at us all.

When school was over that day, Patti's father picked her up in their car. Kate, Stephanie, and I rode home together on our bikes.

As we turned into Pine Street, Stephanie said, "Thanks, guys."

"For what?" Kate asked.

"For going along with Friday," Stephanie replied. "You've known each other since kindergarten, and I've known Patti since kindergarten — it kind of evens things up. See you." She coasted toward her house at the end of the block.

"We've probably let ourselves in for hours of 'the city this, the city that,' " Kate grumbled.

"I don't think Patti's the type, somehow," I said. We'd be lucky if she said anything at all.

"Just wait and see," Kate predicted gloomily.

Friday afternoon after school, Kate, Stephanie, and I rode over to the Jenkinses' house on our bikes. Then we gave Patti a guided tour of Riverhurst, hitting all the high spots. First stop was Charlie's Soda Fountain on Main Street. It has the best chocolate shakes in town and real antique stained-glass windows. Next came Dandelion, a store with great kids' clothes — we tried on stuff for a while but we didn't buy anything. Then we stopped at the Record Emporium at the mall, where you can lock yourself into a booth and play rock music as loud as you've always wanted to. We even stopped by Tully's Fish Market, Riverhurst's answer to Sea World. There's a big pool with fish, clams, and sea urchins living in it and a tank full of lobsters.

"I always feel sorry for the poor dumb lobsters," I said to Patti, "crawling around with their claws tied together."

"They remind me of Japanese horror movies," she admitted with a shiver.

After we left Tully's, we circled Munn's Pond and the Riverhurst Wildlife Refuge. Then we headed back toward Stephanie's house.

Mrs. Green opened the back door as we pedaled up the driveway. "Hi, girls. Bring your things inside. It's getting cool out here." She motioned us in. "Hello, Lauren, Kate — and you must be Patti Jenkins. Stephanie has told me so much about you."

Mrs. Green looked us over with a bright smile. "Stephanie, why don't you take the girls to your room to leave their backpacks?"

We followed Stephanie down the hall to her bedroom.

"Neat room!" Patti said.

"Thanks," Stephanie replied. "It's just like my room in the city."

I jabbed Kate before she could moan.

Stephanie's room is big, with twin beds pushed against one wall. The spreads are striped in red, white, and black, Stephanie's favorite color combination. Two foam-rubber chairs unfold into beds, too — they're covered in red denim. There's a black-and-white rug on the floor in front of the television. She has her own set.

There's also an autographed poster of Stephanie's favorite TV show on the wall.

"He's so cute," Patti said. "But I think I'm taller than he is *already*."

"That's okay," Kate reassured her. "I read somewhere that he likes taller women."

Kate can be very nice.

"Who wants the beds, and who wants the chairs?" Stephanie asked.

"I'll take a chair," Kate said. "The one closer to the TV." She's a little nearsighted, but she hates to wear her glasses unless she has to.

"I'll sleep on the other one," Patti volunteered.

"Lauren, I guess you get a bed," Stephanie said.

We hurried through our pepperoni pizza dinner because we didn't want to miss the beginning of the sci-fi double-feature. We'd barely finished putting sheets and blankets on the chairs for Kate and Patti when the credits for the first movie flashed on the screen: *Invasion from the Ice Planet.*

"Hey — great!" Kate said.

"Have you already seen it?" Stephanie asked.

"Just once," Kate answered.

I'd only seen it once, too, and Stephanie and Patti had never seen it. It's a pretty exciting movie, about an attack on earth by these creatures from outer space who look like icicles. They freeze everything they touch, until all that's left is a small group of scientists in the Amazon jungle who hide in a volcano.

By the time the Earth people had melted the aliens with heat from a giant mirror they built in the volcano, we were all dying of thirst. Hunger, too.

When an ad came on at the end of the movie,

Stephanie bolted out of the room and down the hall. "I'm bringing some snacks from the kitchen," she called over her shoulder.

"I wonder what the second movie is," Kate said as another ad flashed on the screen.

"I think it's about to start," I yelled to Stephanie.

Stephanie scooted back into the room just in time to hear us all groan in disappointment.

"What is it?" Stephanie asked.

"A football game!" Kate growled. "They've replaced the movie with a stupid football game!"

"Bummer. Maybe there's something else on." Stephanie set the tray she was carrying on the rug. I grabbed a handful of chocolate-chip cookies and some Cheese Doodles.

Stephanie flipped past a boxing match, an exercise program, an interview show, and a World War One mini-series — when the TV suddenly lost its color. Above the bare branches of black trees, a white full moon was striped with shreds of gray clouds. There was soft creepy music playing: "Ooooo-OOOOO-ooooo."

"Let's see what this is," Kate suggested. She put down the cheese dip she was holding to give the TV her full attention.

The clouds blew away from the moon, which shone down on a skinny woman in a shawl and a long black dress. The woman had tangled hair and crazy, glittery eyes. She crept through the trees toward an old house.

"Could we watch something else?" I asked quickly. I could tell it was a witch movie.

When I was three years old, I went with my brother, Roger, to see *The Wizard of Oz* at the Riverhurst library. As soon as the Wicked Witch of the West came on the screen, I started to scream. I didn't stop screaming until Roger dragged me out of the auditorium. I know it's silly, but I don't like witch movies any better now than I did then.

"Wait one second," Stephanie said.

The skinny woman pushed open an iron gate and walked up to the dark house. She pointed a scrawny finger at a guy peering out an upstairs window.

"I say to you, Goodman John Hawkins," the woman screeched, "by the powers of darkness, and the bat's wing, and the serpent's tooth. . . ." She stopped and took a deep breath.

Kate and Stephanie were glued to the screen,

waiting for the witch to go on. But Patti had scooted back in her chair.

She and I looked at each other. I don't think she liked the movie any more than I did.

"Stephanie," I said.

"Sssh!" said Kate.

". . . I curse you, and your sons, and your sons' sons, to an eternity of ill luck!" the witch hissed.

"Oh, nooo!" wailed John Hawkins's wife. She was standing at the window next to him, wearing a nightgown and a little cap. "It's the Glover curse!"

Kate and Stephanie both snickered.

"Ill luck!" Kate said. "This movie looks like it was made in 1910." Since she knows how I feel about witches, she added, "Come on, Lauren. It's so old and so bad, it'll be fun to watch."

"Right, and I'll bet Patti agrees with us, don't you, Patti?" said Stephanie.

Imitating the movie, Kate pointed a finger in Patti's direction. "Goodwoman Jenkins," she said in a screechy voice, "I curse you, and your sons, and your sons' sons, to an eternity of ill luck." Then she broke into giggles. "I mean, who could take that seriously?"

Patti grinned nervously, pulling her blanket up to her chin.

"Besides, there's nothing else on right now," Stephanie said.

"Where's the cable guide?" I asked.

"On the bookcase next to my desk," Stephanie answered.

Patti's chair was closest. "I'll get it," she offered.

Patti swung her legs out from under the blanket and onto the floor — and knocked over every single thing on the tray Stephanie had left there.

"Oh . . . wow!" she squeaked.

She quickly stepped back — right onto Kate's backpack. There was a loud crunch.

"Oh, no!" Patti moaned. "I'm sorry!"

"That's okay," Kate said politely, reaching into her pack. "I have another pair at home." Her glasses had broken in half, right across the nosepiece.

Kate squinted down at the mess on the floor. "At least it goes with the rest of the room," she said. "Red juice on a black-and-white rug."

While Kate, Patti, and I picked up cookies and chips, Stephanie mopped at the red circle of cranberry-apple juice with a towel. To cheer Patti up,

Stephanie made a joke. "It must be the Beekman curse," she said in a creepy voice.

Patti tried to smile, but she looked ready to cry. "Will . . . will the spot come off?"

"This isn't anything," Stephanie reassured her. "I'll just flip it over. See? The rug's fine on the other side."

Mrs. Green knocked on the door. "Girls — I'll say goodnight now. Please don't stay up too late."

"We won't, Mom," Stephanie told her.

"Goodnight, Mrs. Green."

"Great cookies!"

Mrs. Green closed the door.

Stephanie switched off the TV set. "Let's play Truth or Dare," she suggested. "Lauren, you go first."

"Patti," I said, "Truth or dare?"

"Uh . . . truth," Patti answered.

"Which do you like better — Riverhurst or the city?"

"Riverhurst," Patti replied quickly. "Much better."

Stephanie looked really surprised, but Patti's answer made a lot of points with Kate. She gave Patti an approving smile.

"Why?" I asked Patti.

"Oh — it's calmer and quieter. And prettier," Patti said.

"But don't you miss the excitement?" I asked.

"Sometimes it's just scary," Patti answered.

It was Patti's turn. "Stephanie," she said. "Truth or dare?"

"Dare," said Stephanie.

Patti thought hard. "Pick up the phone and call . . ." she began.

"Michael Pastore's house!" Kate hissed.

Stephanie likes two boys at school. Larry Jackson, with the ears, and Michael Pastore, who isn't in our room this year.

"Michael Pastore's house?" Patti said hesitantly. She hadn't been around long enough to know who Michael Pastore was.

"Thanks a lot!" Stephanie said to Kate. But she didn't look very upset.

Stephanie sneaked into the hall for the phone book.

"Pastore, B. Pastore, Frank. Pastore, John. That must be it, because it's on Gaton Lane. I just happen to know that Michael lives on Gaton Lane," Stephanie said.

"Isn't it kind of late?" I asked her.

"I took the dare," Stephanie said with a grin.

She dialed the number and tilted the phone so the rest of us could listen. Kate, Patti, and I leaned closer. We could hear it ringing once, twice, three times.

"Hello?" It was a man's voice.

"H-hello?" Stephanie stammered. "I think it's his father!" she whispered to us with her hand over the phone. "Is Michael there?" she asked the man.

"Who's calling?" the man wanted to know.

"Uh . . . a girl from his school," Stephanie answered.

"Please hold on. Michael," the man called out. "Telephone!"

"Coming!" we could hear Michael shout back.

"I can't !" Stephanie shrieked. She slammed the phone down.

We all exploded into giggles.

"Sssh!" Stephanie warned at last. "Mom'll hear us."

"I'd never have had the nerve to do that," Patti said.

"Okay, now it's my turn," Stephanie said. "Kate, truth or dare?"

Kate thought for a while before she replied. For

the truth, Stephanie might ask her something totally embarrassing. On the other hand, the dare could be a really hard one.

"Dare," Kate said finally.

"Ummm." Now Stephanie was thinking. She opened the top drawer of her dresser and pulled out a jar. "I was saving this for a special occasion, but this *is* a special occasion: our first four-person sleepover. Do your hair with this!"

Kate looked at the jar. "Styling gel? No big deal."

"*Purple* styling gel," Stephanie corrected her.

"Purple?" Kate unscrewed the top. "It *is* purple!" She shook her head. "No way."

"You chose the dare," Stephanie pointed out. "Besides, it comes off with shampoo."

Kate stuck her finger into the gel. Taking a deep breath, she smeared the stuff across her bangs.

Her bangs were awesome — a spiky, glittery purple!

"Neat!" I said. "Let me try some."

I dabbed a couple of fingers of purple goop on the sides of my own hair and combed it back. The hair stood out like purple wings on both sides of my face!

Pretty soon, all four of us were crowded around

Stephanie's full-length mirror, dabbing, streaking, and combing.

"I think if I can get this top part stiff enough, I can do my hair like Patti LaBelle," Kate was saying.

Patti Jenkins had arranged her hair into a row of purple spikes, sort of like the Statue of Liberty's crown. Stephanie's purple curls stuck straight out, as though she had had an electric shock.

"That's the last of the gel," Kate reported.

"We look great!" Stephanie declared. "Like we're going to a rock club. I want pictures."

She got out her Polaroid camera and snapped a picture of Kate, Patti, and me. Then I took one of the three of them. Then Stephanie took Kate and me, and I took one of Stephanie and Patti together.

Kate was reading the label on the empty jar of styling gel. "This stuff stains," she said. "I think we'd better wash it out before we get it on anything."

"Okay," Stephanie agreed. "Why don't you go first, Patti? There's shampoo in the shower and towels in the bathroom cabinet."

Patti took her sleepshirt into the bathroom. But she was out in a second. There was a funny look on her face.

"Stephanie," she said. "There's no water."

"No hot water? Let it run for a minute or two," Stephanie told her. "Sometimes it takes a while to heat up."

Patti shook her purple head. "No," she said. "There's *no water at all*."

Stephanie hurried into the bathroom, the rest of us right behind her. She turned on the hot and cold taps in the shower — nothing happened. The water wasn't running in the sink, either.

"The kitchen!" Stephanie said. "We can take turns shampooing each other in the kitchen sink."

We tiptoed down the dark hall to the kitchen.

"Lauren, open the fridge for light," Stephanie whispered.

She pushed up the handle on the kitchen sink. Not a drop of water came out.

"This is really weird," Stephanie said slowly. "It's never happened before."

"Maybe some of the pipes got clogged up," Kate suggested. "Why don't you try your parents' bathroom?"

"Good idea," Stephanie said. "I just hope I don't wake them up. Wait for me in my room."

Kate, Patti, and I crept back into Stephanie's room. We sat in a row on one of the beds, our purple hair glistening in the light.

Suddenly, we heard voices drifting down the hall.

"Stephanie's mom!" Kate whispered. "Turn off the lamp!"

But Mrs. Green switched it right back on.

When she saw the three of us, she shook her head. "Oh, dear," she groaned. "What a mess!"

"Dad says it must be a water main break," Stephanie added gloomily. "It probably won't be fixed for hours!"

Mrs. Green disappeared into the hall. She returned with four old towels. "Wrap these around your heads," she told us. "I hope that will keep the gel off the sheets."

Stephanie dozed with her head hanging off the edge of her bed. I kept waking up, afraid my towel had come undone. Patti was moaning in her sleep. Kate was grinding her teeth. It was a very long night.

The water main hadn't been repaired when Kate and I started home the next morning. Our purple hair was standing straight up. A little of the goo had smeared on our faces, making us look kind of spooky.

"If we're lucky, everyone will be inside having breakfast," Kate said as we sped up Pine Street on our bikes.

But we weren't lucky. Donald Foster was in his front yard, fiddling with a lawn mower. He straightened up fast when he saw us at the end of Kate's driveway.

"*Feeew-wheeet!*" Donald has a loud whistle that practically shatters windows. "Looking good, girls! But where are your broomsticks?"

Kate glowered at him. "Perfect, just perfect!" she muttered angrily. "Remind me never to say 'dare' to Stephanie again."

Broomsticks, bad luck, witches . . . a thought hit me like a bolt of lightning. I kept quiet because I knew what Kate would say: "Lauren, you're letting your imagination run away with you again." I guess that's another way we're different — Kate's feet are always planted firmly on the ground.

But after everything that went on at the sleepover, I couldn't help thinking of . . . the *Beekman curse*. What if Kate's words were right, and the time was right, and the moon and stars were in the right places? Anything is possible.

Especially after what happened on Monday.

# Chapter
## 3

Mrs. Mead had assigned us a paper for English: two pages titled, "If I Taught Fifth Grade." I worked on the paper most of Sunday evening. I threw in lots of stuff about the importance of field trips to make school more interesting. I hoped it would give Mrs. Mead some ideas.

I thought the paper sounded pretty good when I read it over. I wanted it to look good, too, so I typed it on Roger's typewriter.

Monday morning was cloudy and gray. On rainy days I usually ride to school on the bus. But the weatherman on WBRM didn't say anything about showers. "Clearing and cooler," he predicted.

So, after breakfast, I pulled my bike out of the garage and rode up Pine with Kate and Stephanie.

Patti was waiting for us at the end of the street on her bike. We all rode down the hill to school together.

Kate and Stephanie raced ahead. Their bikes were already in the rack when Patti and I stopped at the curb.

I was unstrapping my books and homework from the back of my bike when Patti said, "I'm stuck!"

Somehow she'd caught the cuff of her jeans in her gear chain. I couldn't hold my books and untangle Patti, so I handed my books to her.

The schoolyard was in its usual state of morning confusion with crowds of kids crossing the street on foot, and kids on bikes, and school buses unloading, and cars pulling up to the curb to let kids out. I didn't notice that Patti had set my books down to help *me* help *her* — until she shrieked, "Oh, no! Your books!"

I looked up just in time to see my books and homework zooming away on the back bumper of an old green station wagon.

"Stop!" I shouted.

The driver didn't hear me in all the schoolyard confusion. I jerked my bike back out of the rack (thank goodness I hadn't locked it up yet) and tore down the street after the car. I was pretty sure that the books would fall off the bumper, or that I could catch up with the car at the stoplight on Main Street.

But the books didn't fall off — Patti had wedged them in tightly between the bumper and the station wagon's tailgate. And the driver didn't stop at the light. He turned left before he got to Main Street and kept right on going. So I did, too.

Patti rolled up beside me. "Lauren, I'm so sorry!" she panted.

"We'll catch him," I said grimly, pedaling as fast as I could.

Meanwhile, we were traveling farther and farther away from Riverhurst Elementary School. The green station wagon was showing no signs of slowing down. A right turn, another left turn, around a traffic circle — I was so afraid I'd lose the car, and my books, that I didn't pay much attention to Patti. It wasn't until the driver finally braked that I noticed Patti wasn't behind me anymore.

"See, Patti?" I called over my shoulder. "He's stopping. And my books are safe and sound. Patti. Patti?"

I looked hastily around. Not only wasn't Patti behind me — she wasn't anywhere in sight.

The station wagon turned into the driveway of

a big white house. I skidded to a stop beside the car. The driver climbed out looking as surprised as I was.

"Lauren Hunter!" he exclaimed. "What are you doing here?"

It was Dr. Nadler, my dentist! I'd just been to his office for a check-up, the week before school started.

"Dr. Nadler!" I said. "This is your house?"

He nodded, grinning at me from under his mustache. "I'm only a dentist," he said, "but as I understand it, it's usually the doctor who makes house calls, not the patient."

I pointed to the books sticking out from the bumper. "Those are mine," I said. "My friend put them down on your car just before you drove away from school. She was with me when I started to follow you, but I guess she gave up and went back."

I pulled them out and flipped through the pages. The books were okay. Even my English paper wasn't wrinkled. "I followed you from school," I explained.

"I was dropping off my son, Kevin," Dr. Nadler said. "He's in the first grade this year. I never even saw you." He checked his watch. "Uh, oh. You're going to be quite late."

Dr. Nadler swung open the back flap of the

station wagon. "We'll stick your bike in the car, and I'll drive you back. It'll save you a little time, and I can explain your problem to the powers-that-be in the school office."

"Well . . . that's an awful lot of trouble for you," I said.

"No trouble at all for a girl who had a perfect check-up."

Dr. Nadler lifted my bike into his car and slammed the flap closed. "We'll be there in a jiffy." He opened the door on the passenger side. "Miss Hunter," he said, waving me in.

We didn't pass Patti on the road on the way back to Riverhurst Elementary. I even looked up the side streets for her. No sign of anyone on a bicycle.

She must have turned around, I decided. She's probably in class already. I hope she's explained what happened to Mrs. Mead.

But when I walked into 5B with my late slip, Patti's desk was empty! Mrs. Mead read my excuse and gave me a nod and a smile. "We're just going over our math assignment," she said.

"Mrs. Mead, Patti Jenkins isn't here yet?" I asked.

Mrs. Mead shook her head. "No — perhaps she's out sick."

"Patti was following me on her bike," I explained. "I'm afraid she got lost."

"Let's not worry yet, Lauren. I'm sure someone will direct her back to the school. If she doesn't show up soon, I'll notify the office. Thank you for telling me."

I slid into my chair, dumped my books in my desk, and unfolded my math homework.

Kate's desk is right next to mine. "Where were you?" she whispered excitedly. "One minute you were there, and the next minute you weren't. Where's Patti?"

"Tell you later," I mumbled.

Mrs. Mead caught my eye. "Let's settle down, class. Lauren, would you like to go to the front of the room and show us how you got the answer to problem number three?"

I'd just started to work the problem at the board when there was a dazzling flash of lightning, followed instantly by an enormous clap of thunder. The lights in the schoolroom flickered then brightened. Outside, the gray clouds burst open, and the rain came pouring down.

"Jenny, Mark — please help me close the windows," Mrs. Mead said.

The rest of us stared out at the thunderstorm.

I hope Patti's not caught in this! I said to myself.

We'd finished math and begun social studies when there was a timid tap at the door. Mrs. Mead answered it.

"My goodness!" she exclaimed. "Patti Jenkins!"

Patti was soaked. Her long, straight hair was plastered to the top and sides of her head, and water dripped from the ends onto the floor. Her sweater was so wet that it sagged. Her jeans — light blue when they were dry — looked almost black. She was shivering.

Patti didn't even glance in our direction. She murmured something to Mrs. Mead, and Mrs. Mead said something back. She put her arm around Patti's wet shoulders.

"I'll be right back, class," Mrs. Mead said, "and I expect you to be quiet while I'm gone."

She and Patti were hardly out the door before the room buzzed with whispers.

Stephanie sits in front of Kate and me. She turned all the way around in her seat to ask, "What happened to the two of you?"

I explained about Patti's cuff getting caught, about

my books riding off on Dr. Nadler's bumper, and about chasing his car.

"I lost her, somewhere between the school and Dr. Nadler's house," I said. "I looked over my shoulder, and she just wasn't there."

"You go too fast," Stephanie said. "Patti couldn't keep up with you."

"Did you see how wet she was? I feel terrible about it," I groaned.

"But it wasn't your fault, Lauren," said Kate. "*She* put your books on the car."

I wasn't comforted. "Patti's so upset she didn't even look in my direction," I said.

Just about then, Mrs. Mead came back into the room — without Patti. Patti's desk was empty for the rest of the day. It would be empty for a few days after that, too.

But Stephanie talked to Patti's mother on the phone that afternoon after school.

"Patti's cuff got stuck in her gear chain again," Stephanie called to tell me. "By the time she'd worked it loose, you'd gone around a corner."

"So she tried to find her way back to school," I guessed.

"No, first she tried to find you and the runaway books. She got more and more turned around. It started to rain and there was no one to ask for directions. Finally, Patti saw a school bus a few blocks away. She followed it back to Riverhurst Elementary."

"Is she okay?"

"She's in bed with a cold and a sore throat," Stephanie answered.

"I'll bet the whole family's angry with me."

"No, they're not. Mrs. Jenkins said something about it 'just not being poor Patti's lucky day.'"

After we hung up the phone, I found myself humming — "Mmmmm-MMMMM-mmmmm" — until I realized what the tune was. It was the creepy music from that witch movie!

The Beekman curse, I thought. Maybe this is just the beginning of a lifetime of rotten luck for Patti Jenkins!

# Chapter
## 4

"The Beekman curse!" When I finally mentioned it to Kate, she thought it was the dumbest thing she'd ever heard.

"Really, Lauren!" she snorted. "Three minutes of a silly old witch movie, and you let your imagination run away with you!"

I don't think anything scares Kate.

Anyway, *I* seemed to be having nothing but good luck. I'd gotten my paper back in one piece, and Mrs. Mead gave me a 93 on it. Best of all, not ten days later our class went on a field trip, just as I'd suggested in, "If I Taught Fifth Grade." It wasn't a visit to the wildlife refuge, either. It was a trip all the way into the city, to the natural history museum.

All the kids in 5B, Mrs. Mead, and two mothers

piled onto a school bus at 8:30 that morning. About an hour and a half later, we pulled up in front of the natural history museum.

Even the building is neat: it's made of dark brown stone, with turrets and towers, like a castle. Kate and I hadn't been there in two years, not since Mrs. Beekman drove us in along with Kate's little sister.

"Before we get off the bus," Mrs. Mead called out, "I'm going to divide you into three groups. I'll take one group, Mrs. Mason another, and Mrs. Freedman the third. Please stay with your group as we move through the museum. At twelve-thirty, we'll all meet downstairs in the cafeteria."

Mrs. Mead went through the bus counting, "One, two, three. One, two, three. One, two, three."

Kate ended up in Group One, Patti and I in Group Two, along with Pete Stone and Jenny Carlin, and Stephanie in Group Three — the same group as Larry Jackson, so she was happy.

Kate climbed off the bus behind Mrs. Mead. Patti and I followed Mrs. Mason into the museum. Mrs. Mason is a little nervous, with eyes that blink too much and a choppy way of talking.

"All right," she began. "Let me see." She looked

at a piece of paper and blinked five or six times. "First. American Indians. Right this way. Must stay together."

We hadn't made it through the first room before our group started to unravel. The boys found a big glass case full of live cockroaches, and they were going crazy over them.

"There are thousands of 'em in there!"

"Wow, look at that one — it must be six inches long!"

"What about those slick-looking red ones with the giant feelers?"

"What if they got out of the case?" Pete Stone said, pretending he was going to knock it over.

There were screams from the girls.

"Oh, Pete . . . what a hideous idea!" Jenny Carlin said. But she gave him a goofy smile.

I noticed Patti was staying away from the roaches.

"Awful, aren't they?" I said.

"It's not that," Patti told me. "If I get any closer, I'll probably knock the case over myself."

"What do you mean?" I asked her, although I was pretty certain I knew.

"Like ruining Stephanie's rug, and breaking Kate's

glasses, and sticking your books on that car, and getting lost, and getting soaked. I'm really bad luck," she finished gloomily.

"Patti, you're not seriously thinking about that dumb curse, are you?" To cheer her up I was going to say it was all a coincidence. But Mrs. Mason interrupted.

"Boys and girls! Boys and girls!" She waved her arms and blinked even faster. "Please, please, *please*. We must keep to our schedule."

Mrs. Mason herded us to the back of the museum to look at models of Indian villages for social studies. Then we climbed the stairs to the second floor to check out the stuffed fish and birds for science class. When Mrs. Mason had crossed everything off her list, we talked her into taking us to see the dinosaurs.

Patti stayed a safe distance away from them, too. She was probably imagining the skeletons collapsing into a huge pile of dusty old bones at the very sight of her. We were staring up at a pterodactyl — sort of a giant lizard with wings — when Mrs. Mason suddenly clapped her hands together.

"Oh, dear!" she exclaimed. "It's twelve-twenty-seven already, and Mrs. Mead wants us down in the cafeteria at twelve-thirty." She fluttered her hands anxiously. "We'll have to hurry. . . . Oh, dear!"

We were on the fourth floor of the museum at that point. The cafeteria is in the basement. With four very long flights of stone steps in between, there was no way we could get there in three minutes.

"Um, I think there's an elevator on the other side of the stairs," Patti said in her soft voice. She'd been to the museum lots of times when she lived in the city.

"There is? Thank you. Thank you. Thank you!" Mrs. Mason squeezed Patti's arm gratefully.

The elevator was enormous. "Dinosaurs need a big elevator," somebody joked. It was large enough to hold our whole group, with room to spare.

Mrs. Mason made sure we were all safely inside by counting and recounting heads. She was just about to step in herself when the doors closed soundlessly right in her face.

"Wait!" we heard her cry out.

It was too late. The elevator was on its way down.

"Better press 'basement,' " one of the girls suggested.

Patti reached out and pressed the "B" button. The elevator trembled a little, creaked, and jerked to a stop. Then the lights went out!

"What happened?!"

"Why aren't the doors opening?"

"Did you press the wrong button?" someone asked Patti.

"I pressed b-b-B," she stammered.

"I'm going to try pressing all the buttons," Pete Stone announced.

He brushed past me. Then I heard clicks as he pushed down each button, but nothing happened. The eleven of us were still stuck in an elevator with the lights off.

"I really don't like the dark," Jenny Carlin whined. "Why doesn't somebody do something?"

"Yeah. Get us out of here!" a boy shouted.

Someone started pounding on the elevator doors.

I remembered a program I'd seen on TV about people trapped in small spaces. If one person gets excited, everybody gets excited, and people start screaming or fainting one after the other.

"Hey!" I said loudly. "Let's all calm down. Everybody sit on the floor and be quiet."

"Lauren, was that you?" It was Pete Stone again.

"Yes," I admitted.

"Lauren is right," he said. "Everybody sit down. Mrs. Mason knows we're in here. She'll get help."

We all sat down in the dark. Everyone was pretty cool until Mark Freedman started telling a ghost story:

"Once, a long time ago," he began in a trembly voice, "there was this old haunted house. The man who'd owned the house was murdered. When they found the body, one of his hands was missing. It had been chopped off — "

"Eeeee!" one girl shrieked.

A boy giggled nervously.

"I'm scared, Pete!" Jenny added, scrambling to her feet.

"Real smart, Mark!" Pete said. "Do you want to get everybody crazy?"

Then a man called down the elevator shaft. "We'll have you out of there in just a minute," he said.

There was some hammering, followed by a grinding noise.

"We're moving!" Pete said.

Slowly, slowly the elevator lowered us into the basement. The doors clanked open. Mrs. Mead, Mrs. Mason, and the rest of the kids in Riverhurst Elementary School 5B were on hand to see us pour out.

"Is everybody all right?" Mrs. Mason practically screamed.

"I'm sure they are," Mrs. Mead said.

"Just hungry," said Pete Stone. He caught my eye and grinned.

Jenny Carlin frowned at me. I hadn't really noticed it before, but Pete Stone is sort of handsome when he smiles.

The kids sang songs and told jokes all the way home, but Patti didn't join in. When we got off the bus, she said in a voice even softer than usual, "Lauren, I'm sorry about the elevator. If this keeps up, you won't want to know me anymore."

"Come on — Elevators stop between floors all the time without any help from Patti Jenkins," I said soothingly. "It was time for the museum elevator to break down. True, you happened to be in it when it did, but so was I, and Pete, and Jenny, and Mark, and a bunch of other kids."

When Patti didn't look convinced, I tried again. "Come to my house for a sleepover on Friday. I'll ask Kate and Stephanie, too."

I didn't want Patti to think the Beekman curse had even entered my mind. But of course it had, as soon as those elevator lights went out.

# Chapter
## 5

"The bad luck is all in Patti's head," Kate said the day after the field trip.

Kate and I were hanging out in Kate's backyard, talking things over after school.

"You think so?" I didn't tell her that I was just about convinced the Beekman curse was all too real.

I started to sit down in the swing. "Yuck! What is that?"

As Kate peered down at the ferocious-looking spider lolling on the wooden seat, I heard giggling in the bushes.

"Melissa!" Kate said sternly. "If you don't come and get this spider this second, I'm going to throw it over the fence!"

Kate's little sister scrambled out of the lilacs,

grabbed the spider, stuck out her tongue, and dashed around the house.

"She's got a machine that makes them," Kate said.

I decided against the swing and sat down on a stump.

"Anyway," said Kate, "it's definitely in Patti's head. Knocking over the juice and stepping on my glasses — Patti's shy, and it makes her kind of clumsy. The books on the car — the same kind of thing: she was feeling embarrassed about getting stuck in her gear chain, so she didn't pay any attention to where she was putting your stuff."

"Y-e-es," I said.

"Besides, you got your books back and made a 93 on your paper. What kind of bad luck is that? Getting lost." Kate went on, sounding very sensible. "Of course Patti got lost. She doesn't know her way around Riverhurst yet. Getting soaked — clouds had been piling up all morning, and eventually it rained."

"What about the elevator? She just touched the button, and the elevator suddenly stopped between floors."

"You said it yourself. Elevators are always breaking down. And now Pete Stone is interested in you, which is not exactly bad luck, is it?"

Pete had brought his lunch over to our table in the cafeteria that day. "Hey, Lauren," he said with a big smile. "Any room for one more?"

He'd squeezed a folding chair in between Stephanie and me, and plopped down in it as though he ate with us every day. It was a little embarrassing having him there, but kind of neat at the same time.

Jenny Carlin was sitting two tables away with some other girls. She spent the whole time glaring at me.

"You're right," I said to Kate. "It's good to have a friend as strong-minded as she is. Maybe my imagination had been running away with me. Maybe Patti *was* doing it to herself.

I decided Patti wasn't going to be able to blame herself for anything at the sleepover at my house. I wouldn't leave anything around for her to knock over or step on. I wouldn't let her push any buttons or turn anything on or off. I was going to make my Friday-night sleepover absolutely bad-luck proof.

I asked Kate and Stephanie to help me.

"If the bad luck is all in Patti's mind," I told

them, "then we have to get it *out* of her mind."

"How are we supposed to do that?" Stephanie asked.

"We think of some fun things to do and keep anything bad from happening. I don't think we should eat dinner together," I decided.

Kate agreed. "Too many things to spill."

"Games are good," Stephanie said. "Quiet ones."

"Like Scrabble. Or Monopoly," said Kate.

"I'll be in charge of that," Stephanie told me. "Maybe I'll bring some of my cassettes, too."

"No dancing," I said. "Somebody might pull a muscle."

"And cooking could be fatal," Kate said. "There might be cuts, burns. . . ."

"And having to eat some of the stuff we've made. Remember that disgusting cheese omelette?" Stephanie laughed. "Definitely fatal. It was like a rubber tire!"

"And snacks should have no hard edges or sharp corners," Kate giggled. "They have to be soft or round."

"Best if they're *both*," I said.

"It shouldn't be too difficult to get through the

evening," Kate told us. "After all, it's only a sleep-over."

Since Kate lives closest to me, she was the first at my house on Friday evening.

"Wow!" she said when we walked into my room. "It's so neat, it looks like nobody lives here!"

I nodded, satisfied. I'd taken everything off my lower shelves and jammed it into the closet. I'd shoved all the stuff on top of my desk and bureau and night table into drawers. I wasn't going to take any chances with Patti around.

"It should be completely safe," I said.

"Hey, where's Bullwinkle? I didn't see him in the side yard," Kate asked suddenly.

"Locked up in the spare room," I answered. "He went to the dog groomer today for a bath. It takes his fur forever to dry, and Mom was afraid he'd catch cold outside."

Bullwinkle is our dog — Roger's dog, really. My parents let Roger pick him out at the animal shelter when Roger was five, which makes Bullwinkle older than I am. He's bigger than I am, too. He has thick, black fur, so the people at the shelter told my parents that he was mostly cocker spaniel. As it turned out,

Bullwinkle was mostly Newfoundland. When he stands up on his hind legs, he's over five feet tall. He weighs around a hundred and thirty pounds. He can wreck a room in ten seconds.

"Probably just as well," Kate said. "Now at least we won't have to worry about *him* destroying the place — just Patti."

As soon as Stephanie and Patti arrived, we went into the den. It would be hard to mess up anything in there. The furniture's old — just a chair and a couch, a round coffee table that Bullwinkle uses as a chew toy, and the TV set.

"Make yourselves comfortable," I said to my guests. "I'm going to bring in some stuff to eat."

I'd made a big bowl of my dip, and Kate had baked refrigerator sugar cookies. Mom had bought two extra-large bags of taco-flavored corn chips, pimiento cream cheese, and Dr. Peppers and Cokes.

"I'd like to help," Patti said politely, following me into the kitchen.

"We would, too," Kate said. She and Stephanie rushed after us.

"Okay — we need four glasses," I said. "They're over the sink. . . ."

"I'll get them." Kate flung open the cabinet before Patti could reach it. She took out four glasses. "These yellow *plastic* ones are nice."

"And a tray. It's on top of the fridge."

"Got it." Stephanie lifted the bowl of fruit, pulled the tray out from under it, and set the bowl back down — carefully.

"Some knives to spread the cream cheese," I said.

"*Spoons* are better than knives, don't you think?" Kate suggested.

We made it back to the den without any accidents. We were busy with the snacks for a while.

Then Stephanie announced, "My granddad was clearing out his attic, and he sent us a box of Mom's old stuff. I brought over a game that's kind of fun. It's called Ouija." She pronounced it "Wee-gee."

"Ouija?" We'd never heard of it.

"Right. You ask it questions, and it gives you the answers by spelling things out," Stephanie said. "You put your fingers on this little heart-shaped stand."

She pulled it out of her canvas tote, along with a board with letters, numbers, and "yes" and "no" printed on it. "The heart slides around pointing to different letters until it spells out a word."

Kate sniffed. I could tell she thought it was dumb.

But the game seemed safe enough. Even for Patti.

"Let's play," I said.

I moved the food out of the way. We put the Ouija board in the middle of the table and sat down on the floor around it.

"Okay, each of us has to rest the fingers of both hands very lightly on the heart. Don't push it!" Stephanie directed.

We all placed our fingers on the edges of the heart, Kate with a disgusted sigh.

"Now we have to ask the board what it wants to talk about," Stephanie said. "And really concentrate."

We waited, but the little heart didn't budge.

"I don't understand why it's not working," Stephanie said at last. "My mom and I did it, and it worked fine. She said you just have to have the right attitude."

"Maybe some of us have the *wrong* attitude," I said. I looked straight at Kate, and so did Stephanie.

"All right!" Kate admitted it. "You three show me how it's done."

As soon as Kate took her fingers away, the little heart started to slide.

"It's moving!" I squeaked.

Patti giggled.

"Kate, could you please write this down?" Stephanie asked. "Just in case the answer is a long one."

"There are pencils and some paper in the closet," I told Kate.

The heart moved slowly across the board. It finally stopped with its point on the letter "B."

"Now what?" I asked Stephanie.

"Give it a chance," she said.

In a few seconds, the heart started moving again. The next letter was "O." It hardly paused at all before sliding over to "Y." The last letter was "S."

"Boys!" Stephanie, Patti, and I screamed.

The Ouija wanted to talk about boys!

"Ask it something!" Stephanie said to me.

"Okay." I grinned at Kate. "Who does Bobby Krieger like?" I asked the Ouija.

Kate gave me a shove with her elbow, but she couldn't help being a little interested.

"Concentrate," Stephanie whispered.

The heart slid across the board and stopped at the "B" again.

"Sorry, Kate," said Stephanie. "Who is 'B'? Betsy Chalfin? No, I'll bet it's Barbara Paulson."

"It's moving again!" Patti squeaked.

The next letter was "E."

" 'E,' " Stephanie said thoughtfully. "It can't be Barbara. It has to be Betsy."

The heart moved all over the board before it stopped at the "K."

" 'B-E-K,' " Stephanie murmured. "What kind of name is that?"

Kate leaned forward, waiting for the next letter: "M" . . . then "A" . . . then . . .

" 'N'!" I shouted. "It's spelling 'Beekman,' but with only one 'E'!"

"All r-i-i-i-ght, Kate!" Stephanie said. "Bobby the redhead likes *you!*"

Kate played, too, after that. We asked the Ouija about Michael Pastore, Larry Jackson, Pete Stone — practically everybody at school.

The Ouija didn't always answer — sometimes it just said "no." But it told us that Michael liked Sally Mason — "I thought he had better taste than that!" Stephanie sniffed — that Pete Stone was *not* in love with Jenny Carlin, and that Mark Freedman had his eye on *Patti!*

"Whew!" Stephanie said finally. "This wears

you out. My arms are starting to hurt."

Mine were, too, and my shoulders ached from sitting so stiffly. We took our fingers off the heart — all of us except Patti.

"Can it work with just one person?" she asked Stephanie.

"I don't know," Stephanie replied. "I haven't tried it alone."

Patti murmured. But Kate had turned on the TV, so I couldn't hear what Patti had asked the Ouija.

Slowly, the heart moved across the board. The first letter was "C." Then the heart kind of bounced around for a while, as though it couldn't decide where to go next. It ended up pointing at the "U."

Kate and Stephanie were flipping channels on the TV set.

I held my breath, my eyes glued to the board. The next letter the Ouija gave Patti was "R."

Patti and I looked at each other. I wished she would stop, take her fingers off the heart. At the same time, I think we both wanted to know the worst.

"It's that earthquake movie," Kate was saying to Stephanie.

Then two things happened at once. On the TV,

the earthquake trapped a bunch of screaming sec-
retaries in an *elevator* — and the heart stopped in
front of the "Z."

C-U-R-Z? Then I said it to myself. "Curse!"

I thought I saw Patti's lower lip tremble.

"Oops!" Kate said about the elevator scene. She
switched off the set as fast as she could.

"Hey!" Stephanie said. "I wanted to see that!"

I poked her with my foot and nodded in Patti's
direction.

"Oh. I *didn't* want to see that," Stephanie mumbled.

"Let's go to my room and play Mad Libs," I
suggested quickly.

Kate and I grabbed the food, and the four of us
trooped upstairs. I heard Bullwinkle whine pitifully
as we walked past the door of the spare bedroom.

We played Mad Libs for a while. One person is
It, and she asks the others to give her a noun, a verb,
an adjective, or an adverb. She writes the words in
the blank spaces in a story already written in the Mad
Libs pad. Then she reads the story back.

That night we ended up with some funny stuff,
like "When approaching a *toad* on the right, always
blow your *freckle*." And, "The camp you sent me to

is *slimy*. We go *worm*-back riding every day."

Patti seemed to relax a little.

Then Mom brought in two pillows and two air mattresses from the hall closet. "Good night. See you in the morning," she told us.

"Okay, Mom," I said.

"Good night, Mrs. Hunter."

"Want to look at some pictures? Patti hasn't seen these." I pulled my photo album out of a drawer and opened it to last year's class picture.

Stephanie studied it carefully. "I think maybe I liked my hair better an inch or so shorter," she said, looking at herself sitting in Room 4A, Mr. Civello's class.

"Speaking of hair, what do you think of that haircut?" Stephanie put her finger on Bobby Krieger in the picture and glanced at Kate.

"He's very cute, isn't he?" Patti said in her soft voice.

I smiled at her. Patti was getting as cagey at heading off arguments between Stephanie and Kate as I was.

We looked at photos taken last year at my birthday party, at a picnic, and at a cookout at Kate's house.

Stephanie yawned. "I think I'll rest for just a second," she said. "Where do I sleep?"

"I have the top bunk." Kate spoke up quickly.

She's used to sleeping up there, and I'd told her I didn't want Patti or Stephanie to fall out of it in the night.

Stephanie curled up on an air mattress under a blanket and yawned. "I was up at six o'clock this morning doing the social studies assignment. Poke me if anything exciting happens," she said. Pretty soon she was dozing.

"Stephanie's getting very dull," Kate said.

But I was thinking, We're almost through the sleepover, and there haven't been any calamities.

We changed into our pajamas and finished the food. That was when Patti dropped some dip on her sleeve.

"Better wash it off," I told her. The bathroom is off the hall, next to the stairs. I don't know why Patti opened the door on the left, instead of walking into the bathroom on the right. Maybe she was thinking about something else.

I heard the doorknob rattle, and I rushed into the hall. "No!" I hissed.

But it was too late.

Bullwinkle had been lying in wait for just such an opportunity. When he heard the rattle of the doorknob, he threw himself — all one hundred thirty pounds — against the door. BAM!

# Chapter
## 6

The door flew open with a crash.

"Aaah!" Patti screamed.

Bullwinkle stood stock-still for a moment, his head swinging from side to side, his little black eyes gleaming. Then he hurled himself on Patti. He knocked her down flat and licked her face. Next he romped down the hall toward my parents' room, sideswiping me as I tried to stop him.

"Are you okay?" I asked Patti, who was still on the floor.

"I think so," she groaned. ". . . Knocked the breath out of me."

Mom and Dad's door wasn't closed all the way. Bullwinkle burst through it, and from the shouting that followed, I guessed he'd jumped on their bed.

"Bullwinkle! Get down this instant!" my father roared.

"Lauren!" my mother shouted. "Did you girls let the dog out?"

"Bullwinkle!" I called.

He hadn't been in such demand in ages. Bullwinkle came galloping out of their room.

"Out of the way!" Kate squawked, since Bullwinkle practically filled the hall from one wall to the other with his bulk.

Kate leaped back into my room. Bullwinkle followed. He loves Kate. He proceeded to walk all over Stephanie on the air mattress. Needless to say, she was no longer sleeping.

"Grab his collar!" I said to Kate.

"I'm trying!" she panted.

Kate had thrown her arms around Bullwinkle's neck, and he was dragging her around my room. I was glad I'd put away everything for Patti's visit. There was nothing for Bullwinkle to break, either.

"Slam the door on him!" Kate gasped. "We'll trap him in here!"

It was a good idea, but Roger chose that moment

to come home from his date. Bullwinkle's sharp ears picked up the click of Roger's key in the lock at the back door.

The dog knocked me aside for the second time, ran over Patti again, and hurtled down the stairs.

"Wh-what!" Roger exclaimed. Then, "Bullwinkle!" he bellowed. "You come back here!"

But Bullwinkle had tasted freedom. Paying no attention to his master's voice, he bounded out the door and frisked down the driveway.

By this time, Kate and I had raced downstairs, too, with Stephanie and Patti right behind us.

"Who let him out?" Roger thundered.

"It was a mistake!" I yelled. "Bullwinkle. Here, Bullwinkle. Come get your ball!"

"What ball?" Kate asked.

"I'm lying," I told her.

"Here, Bullwinkle. Nice Bullwinkle. We've got your ball," we all shouted.

Lights switched on all over the neighborhood. The glass hanging lamp in the Fosters' dining room suddenly glowed. "Hey — what's going on?" Donald called out. Across the street I could hear the Martins' baby start to cry. Even old Mr. Winkle four houses down turned on his front porch light.

"Where's the dog?" Patti asked nervously.

"I don't know. Bullwinkle's awfully hard to see in the dark," I said, just before he burst through the hedge and shot off between us.

Stephanie flung herself at him. Bullwinkle knocked her down on the driveway and circled the yard like a circus horse.

Then my mother called from the back porch. "Bullwinkle. Bullwinkle, sweetie." She rattled a food dish filled with Dog Chow. "Dinner!"

The only thing Bullwinkle likes better than running off is eating. He slowed down and cocked his ears in her direction.

Mom shook the Dog Chow again. "Yummie!" she called. "Dinner!"

Bullwinkle trotted calmly toward her, bounded up the back steps, and disappeared into the house.

"Whew!" I said.

"You kids get inside and get to bed!" my father ordered grumpily.

Stephanie was still sitting where she had fallen on the driveway.

"Do you think . . . I could've sprained my ankle?" she said. She touched her left foot and drew in her breath.

"It's all my fault!" Patti wailed.

Before anyone could say anything, she grabbed her bike from the side of the garage and rode off into the night — in her pajamas!

"Patti's left!" I shouted.

"Follow her, George," my mother said to my father.

"I can't believe this!" Roger muttered.

My father ran into the house for his car keys.

"I'm going with you!" I called after him.

"Now, did I hear you say something about a sprained ankle?" Mom said to Stephanie. "Let's get you inside and take a look at it. That big oaf!" she added about Bullwinkle.

Mom took one of Stephanie's arms, Roger took the other. With Kate leading the way, they helped her up the back steps and into the house.

My dad backed the car down the driveway and we turned up Pine Street, looking for Patti.

"She lives on Mill Road," I told my father.

He just grunted. He's not at his best when he's awakened out of a sound sleep.

I'd never driven around town so late at night before. It was dark and spooky. The moon had strips of gray clouds across it, just like in the witch movie.

I wouldn't have been too surprised if a skinny woman in a shawl and a long black dress had suddenly appeared.

Instead, we turned a corner and there was Patti, pedaling for all she was worth in her striped pajamas.

Dad pulled the car up beside her, but she didn't slow down. I rolled down my window.

"Patti," I said, "why don't you let us drive you back to our house? Everything is okay."

She just shook her head.

"We'll drive you home, then," I told Patti as we rolled alongside her in the car.

"Lauren, you'd better stay away from me," she said in a shaky voice. "My bad luck is starting to rub off on everybody!"

Patti began to cry. She turned her face away from us so that we couldn't see it.

"Patti, please stop for a minute," I said. "Let's talk about it."

But she shook her head again. Dad and I followed her home. We waited until her mother came to the door and she was safely inside her house. Then we drove back to Pine Street.

# Chapter 7

Stephanie's ankle was definitely sprained. By the time Dad and I got back, the foot was swollen and was turning sort of blue-green on one side. Mom had called our family doctor, and he'd told her what to do.

She'd set Stephanie up on the couch in the den, so Stephanie wouldn't have to climb the stairs. Mom had made an ice-pack for Stephanie's ankle with ice cubes and a plastic bag.

When I walked into the den, Stephanie and Kate practically shouted, "Did you find her?"

I nodded. "Patti wouldn't come back with us. Now she's absolutely convinced she's bad luck, and she doesn't want it to rub off on anybody."

"That's so dumb!" said Kate.

Stephanie agreed glumly. "Basically," she said, looking down at her fat ankle, "it's just that Patti's a klutz."

"You think so?" I said. "I wonder."

The next morning, Dad lifted Stephanie into the back seat of our car and drove her to her house. When Kate and I went over later, Stephanie was in bed with her leg propped up on a stack of pillows.

"Does it hurt a lot?" Kate asked her.

"Not too much," Stephanie answered. "The doctor said I should stay off it as much as I can for a couple of days. Have you heard from Patti?" she wanted to know.

I shook my head. "I called her house, but her little brother told me she wasn't at home."

Stephanie raised her eyebrows. "That's funny. Patti was supposed to be babysitting Horace today."

"Lauren thinks Patti is still so upset about Bullwinkle's sneak attack that she's avoiding us all," Kate informed Stephanie.

"Hmmm," Stephanie said. "You may be right. But she'll have to talk to us at school on Monday. We'll make her feel better about it then."

Stephanie went to school in the Greens' car Monday morning. Kate and I rode our bikes to the end of Pine Street and waited for Patti to meet us . . . and waited . . . and waited.

Kate kept looking at her watch. "We'd better go," she kept saying, and I'd say, "Let's give her a little more time." Finally Kate turned to me. "You can stay here if you want to," she said, "but I'm leaving!"

We made it through the door of 5B by the skin of our teeth, just as the final bell rang.

"Girls, a little earlier, please, from now on," Mrs. Mead warned.

Kate nudged me as we hurried to our seats. Patti was already in class, her eyes glued to the top of her desk. She looked like she had no friends.

She probably saw Stephanie limping in with her ankle bandaged, and wanted to go through the floor, I thought.

We saved a space for Patti in the cafeteria at lunchtime. But she detoured around us to sit by herself at an empty table in the corner.

"This is serious!" Stephanie declared as we unpacked our lunches. "But I just happened to have a great idea when I was lying in bed yesterday afternoon."

"Oh, really?" Kate said doubtfully.

"The bad luck is all in Patti's mind, right?" Stephanie asked.

Kate agreed. She and Stephanie were agreeing a lot lately. But I thought of the Ouija spelling out C-U-R-Z, and I didn't say anything.

"And Lauren tried to get it out of Patti's mind by not letting anything bad happen at her sleepover," Stephanie went on.

"And it turned into a total mess because of Bullwinkle," said Kate.

"I think the best way to get the wrong idea out of Patti's mind is to put the *right* idea into it," Stephanie told us.

"How are you going to do that?" Kate asked.

"Actually, you're going to do it," Stephanie informed her.

"What?" Kate was flabbergasted.

"Since you started the whole thing — " Stephanie began.

"*I* started it!" Kate exclaimed.

"Of course you did, with your 'Goodwoman Jenkins, I curse you, and your sons, and your sons' sons — ' "

"You know that was a joke. No sensible person would have paid any attention," Kate interrupted.

"May I please finish?" said Stephanie. "All you have to do is remove the curse. It'll be easy."

"Are you crazy? There isn't any curse to begin with!" Kate's cheeks were turning that angry pink.

Stephanie sniffed and swept her hair out of her eyes. "I knew you'd say that, so I came up with Plan B," she said smugly.

"Plan B?" I was all ears.

"You know the book fair's this week," said Stephanie.

"On Thursday. And we're going to have to spend all night Wednesday baking for it," Kate replied. "So what does that have to do with Patti?"

Every year, Riverhurst Elementary has a book fair to raise money for the school library. There's always a theme, and each class has to think of a booth to fit that theme. This year's theme was "From the Pages of Books."

Five-B's booth was a cardboard palace, where we were going to sell the "Queen of Hearts' Tarts." We were all supposed to bake cookies or cakes for it on Wednesday.

Parents help out at the fair, too. Last year my dad and Dr. Beekman took turns sitting in a dunking booth. It was called "20,000 Leagues Under the Sea."

My dad said afterward that he was surprised there was any water left in the booth; he'd fallen in so many times that he thought he'd drunk it all. But the dunking booth made more than four hundred dollars.

Stephanie was still talking. "Since my dad's on the school board this year, he'll be working at the fair. He's going to be a fortune-teller."

"Your father a fortune-teller?" I was shocked. Stephanie's dad is a lawyer, and I don't think I'd ever seen him in anything but a suit and a tie. A fortune-teller in a suit and tie?

Kate must have been thinking the same thing, because she asked, "What's he going to wear?"

"Oh, the usual," Stephanie said breezily. "An old, long dress of my grandmother's, a wig, earrings, and lots of jewelry."

"The usual?" Kate repeated. She and I stared at each other.

"He'll sit in a tent with a crystal ball and look into people's futures," Stephanie added.

"What does that have to do with Patti's problem?" I asked her, as soon as I could get the picture of Mr. Green in a long dress out of my mind.

"He can look into her future and predict nothing

but *good luck*, of course," Stephanie said.

Kate shook her head. "It won't work."

"Why not?" said Stephanie.

"Patti'll know it's your father and that you told him to say it, and she won't believe him," Kate answered.

"First of all, she *won't* know it's my father. She's only met him a couple of times, and he'll be wearing a curly brown wig and tons of makeup. Secondly, the four of us will go in together. Dad will reveal some secrets about all of us, so Patti will be absolutely convinced that the fortune-teller knows what she's talking about."

"What kind of secrets?" Kate asked, suspicious.

"Oh, nothing important," Stephanie said carelessly. "I'll just tell Dad enough about each of us to make it sound good."

I could tell Kate had doubts. I didn't think it was a good idea, either. Stephanie's Plan B would work only if the curse really was just in Patti's head.

"But we have to do something," Stephanie argued. "Look at Patti." Patti was creeping out of the cafeteria like a girl without a friend in the world.

Patti dodged us for the next few days. She rode to school a different way in the morning. She ate lunch alone. She'd get to the bike rack and tear off before we could catch her in the afternoon.

But Stephanie said not to worry. "Mrs. Mead sees to it that everyone works in our booth at the book fair. And that's where we'll corner Patti."

# Chapter 8

Mrs. Mead had posted the list of workers for the Queen of Hearts booth by Wednesday. Stephanie and Kate, Jenny Carlin, and Pete Stone would be in the booth from one-thirty to two. Jenny gave me a smirk when she read it. I would be there with Mark Freedman and some of the other boys from two to two-thirty. Patti was working from three to three-thirty.

Our plan was simple. "We'll grab her at three-thirty," Stephanie said, "and drag her with us to the fortune-teller's tent."

School was over at twelve-thirty on Thursday. All the kids rushed around to the parking lot in back of the building to help set up the booths. Five-B's booth was easy — four big panels of cardboard we'd cut out and painted in art class to look like a palace, with pointed windows to serve through. We nailed the panels to a frame made by Mr. Jasper, the custodian, set the food out on a table inside and were ready to sell.

While Kate and Stephanie were on duty, I watched the first-graders doing a skit of "The Three Little Pigs." Patti's little brother, Horace, was the house of straw. I spotted Mrs. Jenkins in the audience, but I didn't see Patti anywhere.

What if she doesn't come at all? I wondered.

I dashed back to our booth a little before two. Kate handed me the chef's hat decorated with hearts that she was wearing.

"Mrs. Mason is helping out," Kate muttered under her breath, just before she and Stephanie escaped out the back door.

Poor Mrs. Mason. She blinked a few times and worried aloud, "I can't understand why my zucchini bread isn't selling." It wasn't long before I heard a little boy say, "But Mommy, zucchinis are green! I want a gingerbread man."

During my half-hour on duty, chocolate-chip cookies were the favorites, with brownies next. Our booth was one of the busiest. But I noticed that plenty of people were visiting the fortune-teller's tent, too. The tent was plain brown, with silver moons and stars stuck to the sides and a gold scarf flying from the top. A sign on the door said, "The Amazing Madame Mira Reveals the Secrets of the Future. Children 50¢, Adults $1."

Kate and Stephanie came to get me at two-thirty.

"Have you seen Patti?" I asked them.

"Don't worry," Stephanie said. "She'll be here at three. She wouldn't want to get into trouble with Mrs. Mead."

The three of us wandered around, eating egg rolls at "Young Fu of the Upper Yangtze," patting farm animals at the "Charlotte's Web" booth, looking at old junk at "Anno's Flea Market."

We had some fun at the "Three Men in a Tub" booth, throwing wet sponges at Mr. Civello and two other men teachers. Stephanie was so good at it that Mr. Civello asked her if the New York Mets had talked to her yet about joining the team. He's a big Mets fan, so it was quite a compliment.

Stephanie lobbed her last sponge on top of his bald head. "What time is it?" she asked Kate.

"Twenty after three," Kate answered.

"We'd better get into position," Stephanie said.

Mr. Civello and the other teachers cheered when she left.

There was only one way in or out of the Queen of Hearts booth — through the back door. So we just waited in back until the three-thirty kids walked in, and the three o'clock group walked out.

"Hi, Patti," I said.

"From the way you've been avoiding us, we've kind of gotten the idea that you don't like us anymore," Kate added.

"Oh — oh, no, that's not it at all. It's — " Patti was trying to explain.

Stephanie interrupted. "Good! So you'll come with us to check out the fair." She tugged at Patti's arm.

With Stephanie pulling her, and Kate and me walking close behind them both, Patti was swept along. She was inside the fortune-teller's tent before she could even open her mouth to argue.

Before we stepped into the tent, I was so nervous that I was afraid I might laugh and spoil everything. But that wasn't true at all. It was dark inside, except for a few candles on the floor and a dim light shining up through a smoky glass ball. The ball sat on a small, round table. Behind the table was Madame Mira. I kept telling myself it was Mr. Green, of course, but I could hardly believe it: Madame Mira was really eerie.

She was wearing a long purple dress with a high collar. Big silver hoops dangled from her ears, and she had bangle bracelets from her wrists to her elbows. Her dark hair was fixed in a big bun on top of her head, with a silver fan sticking out of it.

Madame Mira gazed steadily at the four of us. Then she spoke in a deep-toned voice with a foreign accent. "Hullo, darrrr-lings. I'm afraid I don't have a group rate."

"Uh. . . ." For once, Stephanie was at a loss for words. She was as spooked as I was by the fortune-teller, and Madam Mira was *her* father.

"No, we're going to talk to you one at a time," Kate replied.

"Ex-x-x-cellent!" said Madame Mira. "Which of you lu-u-uvely gir-r-rls will be first?"

Kate looked around at the rest of us, but no one made a sound.

"I guess I will," Kate replied, straightening her shoulders.

Madame Mira held up a little silver bowl. "Fifty cents, please," she said.

Kate dropped two quarters in the bowl, and Madame Mira motioned her to a short stool in front of the round table.

The fortune-teller looked deep into her crystal ball, moving her hands across it like a magician. "It's clear-r-ring . . . it's clear-r-ring . . . ah, yes! I see a beautiful house. I see a lovely family: father and mother, a wonder-r-r-ful little sister. . . ."

Madame Mira suddenly bent closer to the crystal ball. "I see a young man in your future," she boomed. "A handsome young man with . . . could it be red hair?"

Kate was squirming on the short stool.

One of the secrets Stephanie was talking about, I said to myself.

"His name is commmm-ing to me now. Is it R-R-Robin? No . . . it is R-R-Robert . . . and something with a K. I see you hand and hand. . . ."

Kate leapt off the stool. "Thank you!" she blurted before Madame Mira could say anything else.

Kate glared at Stephanie. But it seemed to be working: Patti looked very impressed.

"Nexxxxt?" Madame Mira waved toward the stool.

I dropped fifty cents in the bowl and sat down.

"Anotherrrr nice family," Madame Mira crooned, peering into her crystal ball. "A beautiful mother, handsome father. A char-r-rming older brother. R-R-Roger, I think, is his name."

Roger charming?

"But wait!" she said abruptly. "Ther-r-re is someone new in your life. Rrrrock, his name is." She fluttered her hands over the crystal ball. "Noooo, Stone," Madame Mira corrected herself.

Thanks, Stephanie, I growled to myself. I was beginning to think Stephanie had gotten a little carried away with making Madame Mira believable.

"I see anotherrrr young lady," Madame Mira went on. "But Stone cares nothing for her. No need to worrrry, my darrr-ling — it is *you* Stone prefers!"

I could feel my ears getting hot. I shot off the stool.

"Come, come." Madame Mira was talking to Patti.

Patti walked slowly toward the table and dropped money into the silver bowl, her eyes on the fortune-teller. But she must have kicked a table leg as she sat down. The table rocked, and the crystal ball rolled.

Before Madame Mira could grab it, it crashed to the ground and shattered!

Patti retreated toward the entrance, horrified by what had happened.

"Wait!" Madame Mira shouted, sounding a lot like Mr. Green. "I'll read your palm!"

"I know what my future is!" Patti cried. *"More bad luck!"* She threw open the tent flap and fled.

"Back to square one!" Stephanie stamped her foot crossly.

"I'm sorry, honey," Madame Mira/Mr. Green apologized. He was picking up pieces of the crystal ball — really a glass globe — and dropping them in the corner. "I tried to grab it, but I just wasn't quick enough."

"It wasn't your fault, Daddy," Stephanie told him. "You did your best." She glanced at the two of us. "Maybe it *is* the Beekman curse."

"Don't start that again!" Kate muttered, a dangerous gleam in her eye.

But Stephanie didn't back down. "Now it's up to you," she said to Kate.

I had to agree. "I think she's right," I said. "If it's all in Patti's mind — as you and Stephanie seem to think — fine. You can put on a show and talk Patti out of it. And if there really is a Beekman curse, only you can remove it."

Kate looked at me as though I were a traitor. Then she turned on her heel and left the tent, too.

# Chapter
## 9

Kate is not a person who holds a grudge. Our phone rang around eight o'clock that night.

"Lauren, it's for you!" my mom called from downstairs.

"Hello," I said.

"Hi, Lauren." It was Kate. "I thought it over, and I've decided I'll do it."

"Do what?" I asked.

"Put on a show for Patti," she answered. "I don't think I'll be ready by tomorrow night, though. What about a Saturday night sleepover? The four of us — you, me, Patti, and Stephanie."

"That's fine with me," I said. "Is there anything I can do to help?"

"Find out all you can about witches," Kate told

me. "And make sure Patti will come."

"I'll call her right now," I said.

Patti's father answered the phone at their house.

"Hello, Mr. Jenkins," I said. "This is Lauren Hunter. May I speak to Patti, please?"

I waited for what seemed like a long time. Finally I heard Patti's voice.

"Hello, Lauren," she said softly.

"Patti, there's a sleepover at Kate's on Saturday, and she especially wants you to be there," I said.

"Oh . . . Lauren . . . I don't think I can. . . ." Patti was trying to think of an excuse. "I have to — "

I wasn't going to beat around the bush. "Patti, the sleepover is for you. Kate's going to *remove* the Beekman curse."

Patti didn't say anything for a while. Finally, I heard her sigh. "I'll come," she murmured.

On Friday, Patti steered clear of us, and Kate disappeared right after school.

"Where are you going?" Stephanie and I asked her.

"To the library to look up some stuff," Kate replied, pedaling her bike toward Main Street.

She was busy on Saturday, too. She called early

that morning to ask if I'd found out anything about witches.

Roger had done a history paper on witches the year before, and I told her what he remembered, which wasn't much. At least it hardly seemed like enough information for a realistic curse removal. "Want to come over later?" I asked Kate.

"I can't," she said. "I have things to do for tonight."

Stephanie and I rode around on our bikes for a while in the afternoon, but it wasn't much fun. Both of us were thinking of the sleepover that evening and wondering what Kate was planning.

At seven o'clock on the dot, I knocked on the Beekmans' front door.

Kate opened it. "They're already here," she said in a low voice. She led me into the living room, where Patti and Stephanie were sitting on the couch.

"Hi," Stephanie said.

Patti gave me a wan smile.

Dr. Beekman stuck his head around the door. "Well, well, well," he said, beaming at us. "This must be Patti Jenkins. First it was the Sleepover Twins," he said, nodding at Kate and me. "Then it was the Sleepover Three." He looked at Stephanie. "Now this group is so big I can hardly keep count. I'll have to call you the Sleepover Friends!"

Dinner seemed to take forever. Kate's little sister, Melissa, did most of the talking, with her mom and dad filling in the gaps.

When it was over, Stephanie, Patti, and I followed Kate to her room.

"How about watching some television?" Kate asked. "There's a horror movie on at nine."

"NO!" Stephanie and I shouted at once.

"Monopoly?" Kate offered hastily.

The four of us played a quiet game, but it was easy to tell our minds were on other things: There wasn't a single argument, not even between Stephanie and Kate.

The clock downstairs struck ten o'clock . . . ten-thirty. . . .

"When are you going to start?" Stephanie asked at last.

"Midnight," Kate answered. "The witching hour."

At around eleven-thirty, she started getting ready. First, she set a dim light in each corner of her room. She had swiped the night-lights from the bathrooms, and she'd even managed to find a pink light bulb for one of them. It gave the whole room a spooky glow.

Next she drew a big circle on her wooden floor with blue chalk. "Right!" she said, stepping back to study it. "I have to get some things from the kitchen."

The three of us sat on Kate's double bed and stared at the circle until she came back. Kate was carrying a tray, but what was on it was definitely not snacks: a cup, a spoon, some dry leaves, a bulb of garlic, and a container of salt.

Kate set the tray down on her desk. She opened a dresser drawer and took out a small bottle filled with yellowish liquid.

"Snake oil," she muttered to herself.

Snake oil? I mouthed to Stephanie.

Kate poured a little of the oil into the cup. She picked up a few of the leaves and mashed them between her fingers. A sharp, sweet smell, like licorice, filled the room.

"Magic herbs," Kate mumbled, sprinkling the leaves into the cup.

She pulled a small clove of garlic off the bulb. She pressed it into the mess in the cup with the back of the spoon.

"Garlic guards against witches," she whispered.

She took a tiny envelope out of her pocket. She opened the flap and shook something out of the envelope into the palm of her hand.

We all leaned forward to look.

"Yech! A spider!" Stephanie exclaimed.

"Dried," Kate said.

Kate added the spider to the cup. Then she looked up at Patti. "Take off your sweater and jeans, turn them inside out, and put them back on," she instructed.

Stephanie and I weren't supposed to question anything Kate did, but Stephanie couldn't help herself. "What's that for?" she asked.

"It turns away bad luck," Kate answered matter-of-factly.

I knew where *that* came from — Roger's history paper. But where did Kate get the rest of this stuff? I asked myself.

Patti had turned her clothes inside out. As the clock downstairs began to strike twelve, Kate said to Patti, "Step into the magic circle."

Patti stepped over the blue line, her eyes wide.

Kate poured a handful of salt out of the container she'd brought upstairs. Then she flung it on Patti.

"Salt's a good luck charm," she explained. "Now,

turn around exactly seven times, without stepping outside the circle."

Patti turned seven times and stopped, looking dizzy.

"Stand on your right leg, and raise your left one," Kate ordered. Patti balanced onto one leg.

Kate took a shoebox out of her closet. "You're going to repeat a verse after me," she told Patti. "I'll say it through first, and then we'll do it a line at a time, together."

Patti nodded.

Kate began:

"Beetle, spider, adder, asp,
Squeeze a toad and make him gasp.
Hear this charm, then say it louder.
All bad luck will take a powder."

"But there's no toad," Stephanie interrupted.

"Oh, yes there is," Kate said. She opened the shoe box and took out a big, fat, gray one.

"Ulp," said the toad, blinking its eyes.

"Hold it," Kate said to Patti, "and repeat after me."

Patti wrinkled her nose, but she took the toad

and held it as far away from herself as possible.

*Beetle, spider, adder, asp. . . .*

Kate and Patti went through the verse together, line by line. The toad wriggled desperately. As soon as she was finished, Patti dropped the toad back into the shoebox, and with a shudder, she started to step out of the circle.

What about the stuff in the cup? I wondered.

Stephanie glanced at it, too.

"Stay there!" Kate told Patti. "There's a little bit more."

Patti paused inside the blue circle. Then Kate handed her the cup of gunk.

"She's not going to *drink* that, is she?" Stephanie blurted.

"If she wants this to work, she is," Kate snapped. "It's absolutely safe."

The rest of the verse went:

*Drink this potion, knock on wood.*
*All bad luck is gone for good.*

Patti made a horrible face, but she drank the potion down, leaves, bugs, snake oil, and all. She didn't complain, but her face became awfully pale. Kate knocked three times on the wooden floor inside the circle.

"That's it," Kate announced. "The end of the Beekman curse."

It was late. Everybody was worn out from the excitement, and no one felt like talking. Patti looked as if she might throw up if she had to say a word. We went right to bed — no Mad Libs, no Truth or Dare.

My sleeping bag was closest to the closet door, and I could hear the toad thumping around in his box.

Wow! I said to myself before I fell asleep. When Kate does something, she really does it right!

# Chapter
## 10

We found out just *how* right Kate does something the next morning. We'd barely sat down to breakfast when the phone rang on the wall behind us.

"Kate, please answer that," Mrs. Beekman called from upstairs.

"Patti, could you pick it up?" Kate asked. Patti's chair was nearest the phone.

"Hello," Patti said. "Beekman residence."

She listened for a moment. "When was Riverhurst founded? In 1703."

"I didn't know that," I said.

"Neither did I," said Stephanie.

Patti was still listening. "I've what?" she said suddenly. "I've *won?*"

Now we were hanging on to every word.

"Dinner for two and the theater in the city," Patti said. She looked around the table. "But there are four of us."

She listened again.

"Okay. . . . Yes, that'd be great! Dinner for four at Tony's Italian Kitchen on West Main Street . . . and free tickets for four to the amusement park on Saturday!"

I hadn't seen Patti smile like that since before she got the Beekman curse.

"Yes, I always listen to WBRH. . . . What name on the tickets? I think . . ." Patti paused. "The Sleepover Friends!"

Patti hung up the phone and beamed at us. "I'd like to say something," she announced. "It's probably silly, but I feel much better about things this morning. Kate, I want to thank you for going through all that last night. I really appreciate it. And thanks to all of you for being good friends and not laughing at me for believing in the . . . curse."

"Oh, that's all right," Stephanie said.

"Last night was kind of fun," Kate told her.

"Hey, wait a minute!" I broke in. "You guys are talking like there was nothing at all to the Beekman curse!"

Kate made a disgusted kind of clucking noise with her tongue. "Of course there wasn't," she said.

Stephanie nodded. "It was just that Patti psyched herself out," she said.

I didn't say anything to that.

"Did you believe in it, too?" Patti asked me, wide-eyed.

When I nodded, Stephanie and Kate shook their heads and snickered. "Lauren!" they both said.

"I know, I know," I told them. "You both have perfectly good explanations for Patti's *bad* luck. But what about this sudden *good* luck?"

"Winning the contest?" Stephanie replied. "Patti's parents are history professors."

"Of course she's used to memorizing dates," added Kate.

"Don't sell yourself short as a witch, Beekman!" I said. "That wasn't the lucky part. The lucky part was having the phone ring at your house *when* Patti was here, and *when* Patti would pick it up! None of the rest of us could have answered the question correctly. How do you explain that?"

"Chance," said Kate.

"Like lightning striking," Stephanie said.

"You can think what you'd like, but have you got any of the potion left?" I asked. "I could use a good grade on that math test next week."

Patti giggled.

"Out of potion," Kate answered. "But how about a spider?" She pulled an envelope out of her pocket and shook a couple of spiders into my cereal. "Chocolate — from Melissa's bug machine."

At that news, Patti let out such an enormous sigh of relief that Kate, Stephanie, and I burst into laughter. And after a second, Patti did, too.

# Pack your bags for fun and adventure with

## SLEEPOVER FRIENDS™
### by Susan Saunders

Join Kate, Lauren, Stephanie and Patti at their great sleepover parties every weekend. Truth or Dare, scary movies, late-night boy talk—it's all part of **Sleepover Friends!**

- ☐ 40641-8    **#1 Patti's Luck**
- ☐ 40642-6    **#2 Starring Stephanie**
- ☐ 40643-4    **#3 Kate's Surprise**
- ☐ 40644-2    **#4 Patti's New Look**
- ☐ 41336-8    **#5 Lauren's Big Mix-Up**
- ☐ 41337-6    **#6 Kate's Camp-Out**
- ☐ 41694-4    **#7 Stephanie Strikes Back**
- ☐ 41695-2    **#8 Lauren's Treasure**
- ☐ 41696-0    **#9 No More Sleepovers, Patti?**
- ☐ 41697-9    **#10 Lauren's Sleepover Exchange**   (February, 1988)

PREFIX CODE 0-590-

# America's Favorite Series

## by Ann M. Martin

The five girls at Stoneybrook Middle School get into all kinds of adventures...with school, boys, and, of course, baby-sitting!

## Collect Them All!

# APPLE® PAPERBACKS

## More books you'll love, filled with mystery, adventure, friendship, and fun!

### NEW APPLE TITLES

| | | | | |
|---|---|---|---|---|
| ☐ 40284-6 | **Christina's Ghost** | Betty Ren Wright | | **$2.50** |
| ☐ 41839-4 | **A Ghost in the Window** | Betty Ren Wright | | **$2.50** |
| ☐ 41794-0 | **Katie and Those Boys** | Martha Tolles | | **$2.50** |
| ☐ 40565-9 | **Secret Agents Four** | Donald J. Sobol | | **$2.50** |
| ☐ 40554-3 | **Sixth Grade Sleepover** | Eve Bunting | | **$2.50** |
| ☐ 40419-9 | **When the Dolls Woke** | Marjorie Filley Stover | | **$2.50** |

### BEST SELLING APPLE TITLES

| | | | | |
|---|---|---|---|---|
| ☐ 41042-3 | **The Dollhouse Murders** | Betty Ren Wright | | **$2.50** |
| ☐ 42319-3 | **The Friendship Pact** | Susan Beth Pfeffer | | **$2.75** |
| ☐ 40755-4 | **Ghosts Beneath Our Feet** | Betty Ren Wright | | **$2.50** |
| ☐ 40605-1 | **Help! I'm a Prisoner in the Library** | Eth Clifford | | **$2.50** |
| ☐ 40724-4 | **Katie's Baby-sitting Job** | Martha Tolles | | **$2.50** |
| ☐ 40494-6 | **The Little Gymnast** | Sheila Haigh | | **$2.50** |
| ☐ 40283-8 | **Me and Katie (The Pest)** | Ann M. Martin | | **$2.50** |
| ☐ 42316-9 | **Nothing's Fair in Fifth Grade** | Barthe DeClements | | **$2.75** |
| ☐ 40607-8 | **Secrets in the Attic** | Carol Beach York | | **$2.50** |
| ☐ 40180-7 | **Sixth Grade Can Really Kill You** | Barthe DeClements | **$2.50** |
| ☐ 41118-7 | **Tough-luck Karen** | Johanna Hurwitz | | **$2.50** |
| ☐ 42326-6 | **Veronica the Show-off** | Nancy K. Robinson | | **$2.75** |
| ☐ 42374-6 | **Who's Reading Darci's Diary?** | Martha Tolles | | **$2.75** |

**Available wherever you buy books...or use the coupon below.**